the last execution

the

A CAITLYN DLOUHY BOOK

last execution

JESPER WUNG-SUNG

Translated from the Danish
by Lindy Falk van Rooyen

ATHENEUM BOOKS FOR YOUNG READERS
New York London Toronto Sydney New Delhi

Everyone wanted to attend that execution.

that day was a day of celebration.

—Hans Christian Andersen, in his diary

the last execution

It is the night before the boy is to be executed on Gallows Hill. He is sentenced to death on charges of arson and the murder of the sheriff's little son with a stone.

It is cold, damp, and black as the bottom of a well in the prison cell, but the boy is not alone. The boy can feel it. There, against the opposite wall. It squats down low and keeps a close eye on the boy. Lifts a hand, and points a finger at him. Laughs at him.

Still in a squatting posture, its tail sticking out like a wooden stake, Satan lurches forward. The boy has not slept a wink, but now he pretends to do so. He remains lying still, even though he can hear the straw being shoved across the floor, then suddenly stop. The boy is so scared he cannot breathe, yet he waits, till a warm stench of rotten flesh hangs just before his nose.

Then the boy strikes. He cannot see a thing, but he swings his arm with all his might. And he hits something. Hard. He hears what must be the sound of a nose being crushed. Feels the blow reverberate up his arm, over his shoulder, and into his chest, before his opponent disappears; it retreats with what can no longer be called a nose.

It is gone.

But nothing has changed. It is the night before the boy is to be executed on Gallows Hill.

It is before dawn on the day the boy is to be executed on Gallows Hill. The first rays of light slowly draw away the dark of night. The dog, which is lying on the ground below the cell window in the February chill, emits a short bark; not so loud that you'd be inclined to chase it down the road on its three legs, but loud enough for the boy to hear it.

The boy must have slept after all, for he has dreamt. He has dreamt of a wide river bathed in light. The boy was driven down the river on a raft. Lying with one hand tucked under his head, he made no attempt to steer, just drifted along with the current, while his eyes followed the movements of plants and animals, color-ful birds, trees with their roots hanging in the water, a rock lizard's unbelievably long tongue. This he watched with half-closed eyes—how a turtle climbed up onto the raft to sun itself at the tips of his bare toes. His brown knees pointed straight up into the sky. Now and then he dozed off.

Now the boy is awake. He knows very well which river it was. The one with all the *s*'s: Mississippi. In America. His father's America.

Mississippi. Exactly how it should be. Long and meandering. And for every *s* on the river, a new adventure. A new opportunity.

It could be his.

Or everything—including all the rest—could be just a dream.

The boy thinks about his father's large blue-red hands. His gaze under the shade of his cap. His voice, in the evenings, in the hills beyond the town, as he lay in a shed or under a bush, talking about America.

〜 〜

"Oh come on, tell me, Dad."

"I can't."

"Ooh, yes. You've done it so many times."

"Quite right."

"Come on!"

"No, Niels. Not now."

His father tugged gently on his elbow to prevent him from sitting up.

"Come on! Tell me about the bison! How big they are!"

"Did I talk about bison?"

"You know very well that you did! When that big gray bull chased after me. You said it would be no match for the bison. That it would've fled like a chicken!"

"Did I promise that?"

"Da-ad!"

His father drew the blanket over him.

"Okay. But this is a bedtime story."

"Yes, Dad."

His father's cough disappeared as he told the story. About their plan. About how they would sail over there, together. The bison, the birds, and the prairies they would see. How they would find a piece of land that was theirs. How the sun would shine, and the rain would fall. How it would all work out. How they would be farmers.

And then the boy couldn't help adding to the dream, till he fell asleep. Later, after he meets the girl, he adds more still, that she is with them in America: When he comes home in the evenings after working the fields, she stands in the doorway of the hut with her long, blond hair. She waves. He waves back. In the hut his father sits in a rocking chair by the fire.

But now the boy catches sight of something strange in the near dark. It is resting on his right thigh. Some time passes before he realizes that it's his hand. The hand is swollen in hues of yellowish blue and red, as though it were a large turnip. He can neither open nor close the hand. It is not a dream. It is as real as the fly that crawls over the hand.

"It's your hand, Niels," the boy says.

He was just a small boy when they walked past a workhouse, but he will never forget it. His father dragged him along, as if he were a dumb household pet; they couldn't pass by fast enough. This just made the boy more curious. He craned his neck to stare. A few shapes sat in the yard weaving straw mats, or arranging some lines of rope. They didn't look up. But when they were almost out of sight, a big man raised his head, and the boy looked into those dark eye-pits, like two black coins. He will never forget that horrid, sucked-in feeling of being able to see right *through* them.

Even when they were long past the yard and he could barely make out the workhouse over his shoulder, his father continued to hurry him along. He pulled so hard on his arm that the boy nearly stumbled.

The chimney of the workhouse had long since disappeared when his father finally slowed down and came to a halt.

"It's like being buried alive," he said.

Now he can feel them. His father's fingers

gripping his shoulder. When he talked about the workhouse. How his whole arm shook, as if he had a fever.

The boy stares at the fly. He cannot feel it moving across his hand.

The hand that set fire to Gorm Pedersen's barn. The hand that threw the stone that made a hole in the blond head of the sheriff's little son.

"I'm sorry," he whispers. "I'm sorry, Dad."

It is close to dawn, just ten hours till the boy is to be executed on Gallows Hill, and the master baker has baked his bread.

He delights in standing there, in the bakery door, with the chill to his chest and the warmth at his back. He delights in seeing the sun leaven and redden out there. It fills him with a dual pleasure: The sun is such a strong and powerful oven that its might cannot be conceived by the human mind, and still he feels that this morning, he's beat it to the post again. It is so big, he is so small, and still he has crossed the line first! This is his delight.

Suddenly he's consumed with fear. He falters.

Recalculates. At any rate, he, the master baker, will abide. Like the first man on the field. A loyal soldier.

"If only we had the right to sell our bread for a bread's price!" he sputters between clenched teeth.

The price of rye has risen. The same goes for wheat. But can one charge *more* for a loaf of bread? No! The Bakers' Guild has tried. The town council—led by the mayor—refuses to budge. Same price. To make allowance for those who can't afford it: the so-called poor. Despite the fact that even fuel has become dearer!

Fuel . . . perhaps this day will prove to be a good bread day after all! He thinks about the beheading of the boy on Gallows Hill; that wastrel, that young arsonist and child murderer.

The master baker summons his apprentice. When the lad arrives, he explains how much bread he should take along and exactly where he should stand on Gallows Hill so he can sell as much of it as possible. The lad nods sleepily.

This prompts a grunt from the master baker. It disgusts him that the lad always looks as if he's just woken up.

"If you don't learn to put in an honest day's work," he says, "I'll have to sell the bread atop Gallows Hill myself—at *your* beheading!"

This remark seizes the boy with fear. The master baker is well pleased. And the boy knuckles down to work.

The master baker is standing in his doorway again, thinking. This thing about the bread prices: It's misguided. The proof is in the lad to be executed today.

One keeps the prices down to accommodate the likes of him. What on earth for? One could ask oneself: If he hadn't had the means to buy the bread—so what? He might have starved to death. Exactly—died his death. The same result as today. Only much, much cheaper. First we waste money by filling his belly with cheap bread, and then we waste money by chopping off his head!

All this talk about *children*. Where does it all

come from, anyway? From overseas? But children don't even count. They're like unmixed ingredients: no substance for a living wage. Children are to be kneaded, formed, and baked. Only *then* can they be called people. Everything else is misguided nonsense. As if one would offer a client a lump of dough when he requests a loaf of bread. *He who sees a child sees nothing.* Isn't that the way it is? It's not like anyone would miss him. Is it really so bad just to say it out loud? What is such a sorry little waif compared with the life-giving rays of the sun?

But then the master baker is interrupted: The first client of the day is a pale girl asking for flour. So she can bake her own bread. He snorts loudly. He may as well donate the bakery to poor folk like her. Then *he* would be the beggar who could come in and buy bread for free! And flour!

"You're going to be the death of me!" he cries.

The girl looks up warily, then drops her head.

"It's my fault," she answers, hugging the flour to her chest.

The master baker is contrite.

"It wasn't meant like that," he mumbles.

He stares after the girl, who hurries off—her frail body, the blond hair falling down around the thin neck.

Just *one* swing. No more, no less to put an end to that frail shape.

It's actually rather strange: You'd think that folk would *lose* their appetite from seeing a head being severed from its body. But no, not at all. Rather the opposite. It's as though everyone becomes insatiably hungry, feels the need to glut themselves with all sorts of bread. But especially the sweet kind, the dear kind. Raisin bread. Ooh yes, the lad should mind to take plenty of raisin bread up to Gallows Hill.

The master baker sees the lad stifle a yawn, but doesn't get upset. He's in good spirits now. When he thinks about it, there are three things that go together very nicely: sunrise, freshly baked bread, and the soft sound of God's big, righteous ax swinging through the air.

One town's many mouths, a chorus fair,
Whilst a head that still doth stare
Rolls to the ground
Without a sound.

There are nine hours till the boy is to be executed on Gallows Hill when the first tendrils of sunlight spread over the ceiling of the cell like a gray-white lake.

The boy is sitting still, looking at it.

He thinks about the time he sat with his father on the hilltop and gazed over it all: fields, forests, lakes, and meadows, and then, the farms. There they lay, spread over the landscape, big and small, as if it were just a game, and each farm was like a card lying facedown on the earth, and when you flipped a card over, the color or number would decide whether you went to bed hungry or not. In the foreground, small people and cows were moving about; in the distance, just the smoke from a chimney top could be seen. But which card should you choose? Which one of those farms would let a wandering father and son work for a meal and a night in a shed?

Noises and gruff little groans came from his father as he tried to find the right posture for his back, but that day the boy barely registered a sound. He was consumed by something else. It was a miracle: He had caught sight of his mother. Although the distance was too great to see her expression, the long black hair and movements were hers. No doubt about it. She was quick yet elegant, worked with haste but twirled around on her toes like a ballet dancer. The boy followed her movements without batting an eye. His heart hammered in his chest; but it would hammer even louder the moment he reached the farm, where he'd seen her, the moment he stepped into the yard and she looked up. When he could see how beautiful she was. But perhaps she'd frown. Perhaps she would purse her lips and say: "*We don't want beggars here!*" But then her mouth and face would freeze. She'd look and look and look at him, with big round eyes. "*Is that . . . is that you, Niels?*" He'd nod, and she'd hold him tight; he'd put his arms around her, too. He would feel she was crying. "*My dear boy, I have thought of you every day—a thousand times a day! You are the first thing I see before me in the morning, and the last thing I see before I close my eyes at night.*" He'd say: "*Me too.*" She would kiss his face. It would be wet with her tears. He'd say: "*I always knew that I would find you!*"

"Shall I choose?"

Niels startled, interrupted. His father looked at him searchingly. He'd meant: Which farm should they try? The boy looked back at the farm where he'd seen her. The magic was gone. He no longer thought that the woman there moved so gracefully. Wasn't that more like a waddle than a walk as she walked away? Now you could see that it wasn't black hair, just a black cloth she'd wrapped round her head. It wasn't her. His father could sense something was wrong.

"What are you thinking about?"

"Nothing."

"Yes you are. Tell. What?"

"Nothing special."

"Who?"

The boy knew it well enough. His father had told him a thousand times: His mother had died when he was born. This he knew all *too* well. He could live, and she died.

Niels grabbed a stone, jumped up, and threw it with all his might in the direction of the farm with the false mother. But the farm was twenty throws away, perhaps more. The stone landed a little farther down the hill, bounced a couple of times, and disappeared into the grass. His father misunderstood.

"Shall we try *that* one?"

"No!" The boy pointed at random to a farm in the opposite direction. His father looked at him again.

"*They've* got work," he said. "I'm sure."

"I think you're right," answered his father, getting up.

Niels could see he was in pain. His father tightened the rope around his waist and put a hand on his son's shoulder.

"You know what? I think tonight we'll have roasted lamb!"

All at once the boy realized how hungry he was. He forced himself not to look in the direction of the farm with the woman. As they went down the hill, he tried to focus on their goal: getting a job. If he didn't think about anything else, it would work. Just think about the one thing. Just hear the one sentence: *Yes, we have work.*

The farm was in better shape than you could glean from the hilltop. The boy had learnt to interpret the tiniest clues—what would increase or decrease their chances of getting to work. First and foremost, the farm may neither be too slick nor too shoddy. If it was too pretty, it meant they didn't need help—not even to sweep the yard. And if everything was too run-down, it meant that the owner either was in a fix or just couldn't care less. Both scenarios had the same result for father and son: no work.

That day the boy couldn't rid himself of the sinking feeling: This farm was a tick too neat. He wrung his cap in his hands hard, as if the desire for a job lay hidden in its folds. *Come on! Say yes! Say: "Yes, we could use an extra couple o' hands." Say yes!*

The farmer came out of the stable, and the boy's dad stepped forward to present their case.

"Do you have work for two men?"

The boy stood to attention, strained every muscle, each and every brain cell: *Come on! Yes! Say YES!*

"The lad doesn't look like much . . . ," said the farmer.

That hurt. His whole body felt all warm-like and numb, even though he tried to stand on his toes and spread his shoulders. He felt he'd let his dad down—by not being bigger, taller. By not looking like much.

"We've all been small," said his father.

"True enough," answered the farmer, "but that won't bake us any bread." The farmer smiled weakly, but his father didn't flinch and looked him straight in the eye.

"But isn't it by hard work that we grow taller?" he asked.

The farmer's gaze faltered for a moment. He glanced from father to son and back again.

"Perhaps you've got a point. . . ."

And then they were given a chance. *Yes*, they could stay. *YES*.

They were to gather stones. His father pointed to a large stone, but as Niels managed to get his fingers in under it, he realized it was going to be far too heavy. Out of the corner of his eye he could sense the farmer watching him from a distance. He managed to heave the stone onto his lap, and then he tried to walk on casually, pursing his lips in a soundless whistle to hide the effort of it all. Once they had rounded the edge of the barn, his father stepped forward and grabbed the stone, just before it slipped through his fingers. He cast his son a quick smile from under his cap: They'd found work.

This was their life. As he sits in the prison cell, the boy thinks about it all.

He was still quite small when he first asked about his mother; he was still quite small when he stopped asking about his mother.

His father wouldn't have it. Not that he ever said so. There was no need to. Even when he couldn't see his father's face hidden behind the worn cap, the hair, the already bent and buckled back. His body said it all: that now there would be no more talk about that. Else it would be impossible to work. To keep going.

He knew two things about his mother: that she'd died when he was born and that her hair was black. That's it.

At first he'd simply stared long and hard at all women with black hair. Later it happened more fleetingly. It had always been just the two of them: father and son. They tried to get by. Find work. Find food. Avoid the law.

"Remember. We're on our way home," his father always said.

If a policeman stopped them, Niels should lie. He should tug on his father's sleeve and ask when they could go home, when they could sit in front of their warm oven. Even though they'd never had an oven. Even though they'd never had a house. Or a place to spend the night. Otherwise they'd be sent to the work-house. Because their kind wasn't wanted loi-tering 'bout town. Their kind stole, or begged. Nor were they a pretty sight.

And the workhouse. That was the worst. His father, shaking as if he had a fever, had said: "It's like being buried alive." The boy would never forget the man who'd looked up with eye-pits like two black coins you could look right *through*.

If they were lucky, they slept in barns. If not, in all sorts of places. In summer, under the stars; in winter, in deserted sheds or under a clump of bushes. Here they would lie, talking about America.

They rose early in the morning and looked for work. Any kind of work. The men squinted at a thin boy and a father's bent back. They shook their heads or turned their own backs, without a word. But now and then there was a nod. A nod that meant that now they could get on with it. Like that day with the pile of stones. Or those days they could do something else, take care of something else. Drain marshes. Cart away waste. Work. Live.

But first they had to get a grip on things. In his mind's eye he could see how his father tugged on the cord of his pants in an attempt to fasten them round his thin waist. How he pulled a face. That seemed to help. It was as though the pain in his stomach and the pain in his back balanced each other out in some way when he pulled on the cord. Until the work was done.

His father worked at an even pace. Barely a break, barely a word. As if he daren't stop. He kept going—more and more bent—until the pile of wood or stones was gone.

The boy looked away once their work was done, looked away when his father tried to straighten his back. Shift it into place. The boy never did so, but he wished he could cover his ears with his hands, so he didn't have to hear the sounds his father made. But it was always the same. The sigh: *"Jaja."* When it was all over. When he could function again. They took turns sipping from a water flask. *"Jaja."*

The boy can hear the dog on the other side of the prison wall. It is whimpering softly. Either it's in pain or it's uneasy. He says it.

"Jaja."

He doesn't know if the dog can hear him, but it seems to settle down.

The boy can see his hand a little better now. He tries to move it. That's not good. The fly is still perched on what looks to be the back of his hand.

Niels starts thinking about the girl again, although till now he's tried not to.

That day he had met her in the field, a fly,

like this one, kept landing on her lip. Again and again. How she had laughed. How she looked at him. How she tossed her head and ran her fingers through her hair—quick, quick, slow. And then the fly again. And the laughter.

"Do you know that fly?" the boy asks now, looking down at his hand. "Is it sitting in the pub bragging its head off?"

The boy remembers how they had tossed burs at each other. The kiss this led to.

White shards of pain shoot through the boy's brain. He'd accidentally bumped his hand against his knee. They dart from the back of his head, to the left temple, and across to the right. The boy bends forward, tries to breathe deeply, eyes closed. He remains in this posture for a long time.

"Now he's thinking about the girl," says the fly. "Oh, for heaven's sake, now he's thinking of that blond lassie again!"

Niels concentrates on the pain. *Or else I'll disappear*, he thinks. *Or else, I'll disappear.*

The fly is tripping about on the hand in

silence. Now it stops dead in its tracks.

"Dare we suggest that the lad think about something else?" says the fly.

Then it struts on. Halts in midstride.

"That he thinks about something else . . ."

"But what?" whispers Niels.

"What? What! What?" squawks the fly. "As if there weren't anything else to think about! What a waste of a life if there were *nothing at all* worth remembering. Think! For example: How 'bout that time the lad got a peek in that fat book about America?"

"That time my foot got run over?" Niels asks.

"The time the lad's foot got run over by a cart; it recovered, though—*the foot*—and the rich man invited father and son to his home, and they got to sleep in the loft," says the fly. "But before that, they paged through a book about America. There was a chapter about the Mississippi River."

Now the boy understands that the fly is talking to the hand.

"Take the crocodiles in the Mississippi, for

example," continues the fly. "You can't always see them, but they're there. The crocodile floats in the water like a log—its eyes like knots in a tree trunk—till the cow tries to cross the river."

"That was shown in the book," says the boy.

"I know *that*!" says the fly. "The crocodile lies absolutely still, *until* the cow comes down to the bank of the river."

The boy says no more.

"Then it shoots out of the water, mouth open wide. It digs its hundreds of sharp teeth into the cow's neck and pulls it down under the water. *Swoosh*," quips the fly. "The water is churned foamy-red. Round and round. One second, then everything is quiet again. The Mississippi is as calm as before."

The fly turns on its heel again. Halts in mid-stride.

"That's a story from the real world," it says. "Now it's over. *Bam!* Easy-peasy, over and out! That wasn't so hard, was it?!"

The hand seems to chuckle to itself.

It is morning, the messenger posts the notice of execution in the town square, and—for those who can read—it is stated: THERE ARE EIGHT HOURS TILL NIELS NIELSEN WILL BE EXE-CUTED ON GALLOWS HILL.

The mere mention of his name sends a chill down the messenger's spine. It's a blessing he's finally been caught. The messenger had heard that the man was mad. That he was prone to violent, insane behavior. Set ablaze everything within his reach. Watched folks' homes burn down to the ground while he stood idly by, hissing a demonic laugh.

Not to mention the murder of the sheriff's

son. The messenger had heard that the man had held the little lad down with just *one* arm while he had hammered away at his head with a stone, and the child's cranium burst like an egg, his brain trickled out like yolk!

That the likes of *him* had gone free among men! The messenger gets the shivers just thinking about it, the thought that it could have been *him* who met that man on a deserted country lane late one night. It could just as easily have been the messenger ending up in a ditch with a cracked skull or a slit throat!

The messenger senses at once that someone is lurking behind him. Even though he knows it's just his imagination, he can't help but peer over his shoulder. But there *is* someone. Someone watching him. There, in the shadows of the goldsmith's house. His heart beats faster. Then he sees it: It's a thin girl. She's shifting from one foot to the other with something clutched in her arms. Perhaps she's waiting for someone?

The messenger thinks she's a fallen woman.

That she has gotten herself pregnant. And she's waiting for the father of the child, but the father doesn't show. The messenger thinks this because she seems so desperate. She's not sluggish like the others on the town square. And then she stares at him. As if she needs his help.

He yells at her, which only makes her draw back into the shadows.

"What's your name?!"

She doesn't answer; but she doesn't flee, either. The messenger is confused. He has the feeling that this is what he's been waiting for, that this moment is essential to life at large. It is now he must do the one and only right thing.

"The executioner is coming all the way from Odense city," he finally says. "That's why it's going to be so late."

He doesn't know why—of all things—he chooses to say this, whether it's the right or wrong thing to say. The words come out of his mouth, but it isn't him who speaks. He goes on, regardless.

"A whole lot of people are coming to watch.

A whole lot," he says. "But I'm sure that if you stand up real close, you'll be able to see the chop quite clearly."

The girl doesn't answer, and the messenger can't tell if he should say any more. He considers offering to arrange a spot for her in the front row. In a flash, his brain imagines how he leads her through the masses: He clears the way before her up to the scaffold, his goal. And he is sweating heavily as he forces his way through the crowd with elbows, shoves, and calls of authority. He leads her by the hand on the final stretch. He feels as if everyone steps aside of their own accord, and they make it to the front of the crowd in good time to see the swing of the ax. And then she turns to him and smiles. Her face and dress, her protruding belly, are splattered with rancid blood and gore. *That should take care of it*, he thinks. *That's taken care of.*

The messenger is back on the town square, where his heart skips a beat, and he is struck by an insane idea: He is the father of the child!

Just because he's had those thoughts. About doing it. Doing it with Signe from next door. Doing it with other girls—and now, with this lass here.

The bad conscience wells up inside him. There is so much to be taken care of, so much work to be done. He has dallied on the square for too long, and thought about *it*. He's got to get moving! Still, something holds him back. A desire to drop everything he has in his hands. To run to the girl in the shadows. To rob the goldsmith's! But he's being pushed and pulled from all sides—being borne down. He can hear the scolding he will receive in the course of the day, feel the raps on his knuckles; he is utterly aroused, yet tired as an old man.

"Then it could be all the same!" he exclaims.

It's not due to anything in particular—not that he can tell, anyway—but now he is near to running down the road.

With every step the messenger gets more and more agitated. He is resentful and angry, and he directs the brunt of his anger at that man on the poster, the man who is to be executed. The messenger will be there, all right! He'll buckle down the whole day to make sure of it. Then he'll fetch the Smith brothers. They'll need to get over to Gallows Hill in good time. Then they'll be ready. They can stand right up front, in the first row, and shout. They can yell at him, spit in that demon's face! He'll take his knife along. He imagines that he slices an ear off the severed head and hides it, before anyone sees. That he keeps it wrapped in a rag; and that one fine night he gives it to someone or other, who looks at it with flushed cheeks, until she leans her body into him, and they lie down in the corn together. . . .

Once the messenger has disappeared, the girl dares to come out of the shadows and walks up to the notice of execution. She is standing with her package in her arms. After she has stammered her way through the notice, letter for letter, she disappears.

One town's many mouths, a chorus fair,
Whilst a head that still doth stare
Rolls to the ground
Without a sound.

It is seven hours till the boy is to be executed on Gallows Hill, and now he can hear that he is not alone in the world. The sound of a carriage on the other side of the cell window, its bars radiant with evaporating frost; a rummaging somewhere in the building; a door that opens, or closes; a final shuffling of steps, coming closer. The sound of keys in a lock.

The warden is carrying a bucket. He yawns. Then he stops and stares, mouth open wide.

The fear in the warden's face when he spots the boy's hand—it makes the boy lower his head to his chest. As if this could make the fear disappear. The boy remains sitting in this posture. He doesn't know what else to do. To prove that he doesn't have coal-red piercing eyes. He hears the warden's ragged breathing. The boy is quiet as a mouse. Waiting. Until he hears a cough, several coughs, and jangling keys as the warden retreats.

The warden has left the bucket standing outside the cell, but close enough that the boy can stick a hand through the rails and reach. They both know that the warden does not want to get too close.

"It's not true," says the boy. "That is not who I am."

The stone knocked against the inside of his teeth. His tongue could shift it from side to side so it made a little melody. The boy doesn't remember how old he was, just that he'd become taller now, his father shorter.

He remembers that he was very hungry. That was why he had the stone in his mouth. To take the edge off the hunger.

It had been days since they'd had work. A place to sleep. A decent meal to eat.

The last time they'd had some money, his father had used it to buy a bottle of brandy. There was no mention of it. It was for the pain—the boy knew—but he couldn't say it. It was autumn. The wind cut into his skin. They were frozen to the bone, even though they were walking.

"What's winter like in America?"

His father didn't answer.

"Do the birds fly away? To the south?"

"I don't know."

"Or do they stay?"

"If I could, I would," answered his father.

"Tell."

"Let's wait, Niels."

"When, then?"

"Can we decide?" asked his father.

"Yes, don't we always decide, Dad?"

"That's settled, then."

"When, then?"

"It's up to you."

His father stopped short, busied himself with tightening the rope around his waist.

"Okay, then," answered the boy. "After that tree on the barrow!"

His father nodded.

The boy is thinking about the rope around his father's waist. Soon there would be no more than a tight knot, so thin was he. Sweat broke out on his father's forehead each time he pulled the knot a little tighter.

But once in a while the boy felt a glimmer of hope. Like one time they found work: His father got a shilling from the farmer. But best of all, when they were done, the farmer's wife brought two steaming-hot mugs out to them. They stood and drank outdoors like two weary-worn comrades as the warmth spread into their chests. The boy felt himself stretching several inches in height. Even his father could feel it. It was as if his back had unbuckled. Never had the boy seen him stand so tall.

Then followed three weeks of nothing. And

after one night spent in a stand of reeds, his father was pitched down into the ground. There his back stayed put.

Niels walked up to the road; his father lay in a deserted barn because of his back. Niels waded into a field and sat down. He looked like a tall local lad, who sat gazing over the yellow-green landscape, daydreaming about things big and small.

He listened for the first sounds of a wagon that would meander its way along the country road: At first, barely the buzz of a bee. Then it became a distant rumbling, which seemed to come and go, yet still mounted evenly. Like his heartbeats, which quickened in time with the beat of hooves. And finally, the voices of people and their possessions. He forced himself not to look in the direction of the wagon when it came closer; but he was like a feather, light, ready to jump up and spurt down to the road. In that instant she called to him.

Niels imagined that his mother sat in one of

those wagons. That she suddenly caught sight of him, there in the field. *Stop*, she would cry. *I said stop, dear man!* The driver would yank on the reins, and she would sway to her feet, so tall and beautiful. She would call: *Niels! Is that you, Niels?* And he would turn his head; as if plucked from thought, he would smile and say: *Yes, Mum, it is me.*

That day, four or five wagons passed him. Without stopping. Only one called to him. A man: "If you were living under my roof, I'd take the whip to you!"

When Niels got back to the barn, his father was lying on the ground, mouth open wide. He was sleeping with one hand on his chest, the other wrapped round the bottle.

The boy gets up from his seat on the floor. The mere fact that the battered hand must get up with him makes the room swim before his eyes. The fly takes flight, and Niels nearly loses his balance. He waits. But he's so weak, he must lean against the wall. This surprises him.

That his legs, for example, aren't stronger. That cannot be. But the first step is an explosion up into his body. Nails scraping to grip the wall, mouth sucking in air for his lungs. The lights cut into his brain.

"So who says you can't remember anything from when you're born!"

It's the fly talking again. It takes a while for the boy to focus. Then he locates the fly against the opposite wall.

"Hah! How can it be, then, that the boy can remember he sat with his mother in a garden?" asks the fly.

Yes, he can. Niels is sure. He can remember that she sat in a garden with him. She sang for him. Perhaps they had a few days together, before she began to bleed. Before she died.

The hand seems to buzz with applause.

"Just like the painting," says the fly.

He can remember it now. It hung on a wall.

"It pictured a mother and child," he says.

"Exactly!" cries the fly.

"She's sitting with the child held close to her

body, one hand on his head, the other on his stomach."

"Well done!"

"The child is sleeping, but she is awake. Her cheek is resting on his head."

"Precisely!"

"They are wrapped in a blanket of some kind. It's just the two of them."

"Yup!"

The painting hung on a wall somewhere. Somewhere he had been.

The boy moves closer to the prison rails. He fills his good hand with water, moves slowly toward the light, whistles softly, reaches up, and lets the water flow out of the window. A bark in reply. He hopes this means the dog is drinking. He repeats this three times.

The fourth time, he lets the water run over his own scorched lips. The water burns down his throat. Then he sits down again.

Something else comes to mind. It surprises him that he can remember something like this. What he remembers is: If you pour a bucket of water into one end of the Mississippi, it takes a year for the water to reach the other end.

He says: "One year is a long time."

He sees the almost infinite succession of days snake before his eyes.

He sees the road before his eyes; he links up with the girl.

"Now he's thinking about the girl again!" exclaims the fly. "Will he never be the wiser? Hasn't he burnt his fingers often enough?"

The hand is buzzing, as if it's enjoying itself immensely. It's buzzing like a beehive.

Then he remembers what happened one autumn night, when they had walked along a country road, he and his dad, dead tired. They froze. They were hungry. The boy could feel it, and it gnawed at him: the sweet desire to give up, just to lie down for a while. He didn't say it, but he thought: *Let me lie down in front of the workhouse.* He would never say it out loud, but it seemed as though his father could sense it.

"Just a little farther, my boy."

He rested a hand between his son's shoulder blades.

"Just over that ridge, Niels," he said. "There lies a barn so fine! Just for us. You wait and see!"

If those large blue-red hands could have transformed themselves into a pair of wings, they would have.

As he and his father came over the ridge, the sky was red. A fire so big was burning. It was someone's farm. And as they came down the slope, they could see them: the family. They stood together and watched their home burn down. The boy wanted to stop, but his father urged him on.

"It's hard enough as it is," he said, and walked right past them.

Now the boy realizes he is crying, and that he's been crying a long time.

"This is not who I am," he says.

It is six hours till the boy is to be executed on Gallows Hill, and as the winter sun wedges itself between the houses on the market square, the master carpenter arrives with a very long rod.

He casts a long shadow before him, and he feels the anger right into the tips of his fingers, which are tightly clasped around the measuring rod. Had it been *his* business that lad had set on fire, he would have severed his head from his shoulders himself—with his very own saw!

The sound of his heavy steps prompts a dog to come around the corner, stop, and whimper softly. Well, at least the remains of a dog. The master carpenter casts the three-legged cur a sidelong glance.

"Shoddy workmanship," he mumbles.

He can't help but see the dog in this way. As if it were a chair. Arsonists, child murderers, and three-legged mongrels! Isn't it about time the town council did something about the state of affairs? The town is a three-legged chair about to topple!

The master carpenter spits a glob into the dog's coat. It is so dirty, it could be all the same. The dog doesn't move. But as the master carpenter takes a swing at it with the rod, it bolts—with surprising agility for a crippled cur.

But now the master carpenter stops in midstride, smiling to himself, as a thought strikes him. The solution: a legion of men armed with rods. Instead of a council that just sits around arguing about trivialities, eating lavish dinners, and failing to make decisions about anything at all. He sees himself as their leader.

How they march up and down the streets. Sees how they drive thieving boys, beggars, and malformed creatures out of town. The plan is as simple as it is ingenious. Cash on demand. A blow with a stick is a language that everyone can understand. Now he can see the children of the town before him, cheering as they advance through the town, their rods held up high.

It's not the sound of the warden opening the cell door to let him in, but perhaps it is the sound of the lock turning in the second door that triggers it: The idea of an army of rod-bearing men disappears, his anger dissolves in an instant, and in its stead the master carpenter feels a rush of fear. Is the world really on the brink of ruin? Is the Day of Judgment upon them? And will the murder of a master carpenter be the next grain of proof the towns-folk can talk about?

The master carpenter feels the tension in his neck. How his muscles cramp. He is a big man—bigger than most—with muscles well accustomed to use. The warden is hardly the smallest of men either.

There are two of them, and he's just a lad, thinks the master carpenter, as they walk down to the prison cell.

When he sees the boy, his fears are checked at once. He imagined him to be somewhat bigger. Bulkier. Older. He is not big. He is thin—surely due to a lack of food—but also due to a slender frame. Not a dimension that should give rise to alarm.

And yet he feels a certain unease: That lad standing there. There is something amiss. But you couldn't *see* it if you were to meet him on the street. Could you? Perhaps that's it. That he is neither child nor man, but something else entirely. Something or other. You would think they were born without parents! Could this be the core, the ruin of the entire town? Is that—there in the prison cell—merely one out of a horde of unruly miscreants that roam the town like hardened criminals?

Yet in the midst of this muddle there is one

thing that still makes sense: money! The master carpenter's trepidation disappears as he thinks of his fee. Coffin and price. In the lad's case there's certainly room to make a profit. He gets a fixed price on the coffin—irrespective of size—so here there's timber to be saved!

Now the warden asks the condemned to rise. He complies without a word, albeit somewhat slowly. *It is just a boy*, thinks the master carpenter. But still the warden keeps a wary eye on him as the master carpenter marks off his dimensions on the measuring rod.

That's odd, thinks the master carpenter. This is usually when the condemned react. When they realize he is taking measurements for their *coffin*. Then the ax and the earth, the hungry mites and the insects, become clear and near as day. Some break down and cry, others begin to scream and shout, call him names; a few just cling to the rod, as though *it* could prevent them from dying. On one occasion the condemned man refused to let go—no matter what—and the rod broke. But of course he got his head chopped off as planned. He was simply buried in a coffin spied to size.

This boy is different. He stands still in silence. Even holds his breath, as if he is loath to be a burden.

A fly lands on the rod; now the master carpenter spots the boy's hand. It looks bad. As if it had been crushed under a pile of logs, as if wild horses had trampled all over it. Oh well, not too mashed and swollen to be stuffed in a box. The master carpenter has all the measurements he needs, and he is keen to leave before he can have any regrets. But as he turns to go, the boy opens his mouth after all.

"Pardon me," he says. "May I ask you something?"

The master carpenter doesn't answer and he ducks behind the prison bars.

Then the boy asks: "Why does a raft not sink?"

The master carpenter waits to see the warden turn the key in the lock so he can answer without regard to the condemned's reaction.

"It's a question of weight and displacement," he answers. "And buoyancy."

The boy seems to think this over for a moment before he asks: "What kind of wood should you use?"

"The harder, the better," answers the master carpenter.

"The harder, the better," repeats the boy.

"So the water can't get into the wood," explains the master carpenter.

Now the boy looks at him for the first time. The master carpenter feels a pang as the boy lifts his head.

"Thank you," says the boy.

Then he drops his chin down to his chest again.

As he steps out onto the town square, duly marked-off rod in hand, the master carpenter catches a glimpse of the three-legged dog, which is limping round the corner.

He thinks of the strange circumstance, that someone who has burnt to the ground a barn that was made of a lot of timber is soon to end in a coffin that is made of a few planks of wood. He falters a moment, looks uncertain of the direction to take, when he is struck by the thought underlying his first: *What kind of life is this?* He stops short, seized by exhaustion.

It is not a memory that the master carpenter immediately recognizes as his own, but now it manifests itself like a perfect joint: He can't be more than a young lad; he is in a tavern; it must be a celebration of sorts. He is sitting on the floor, watching a game of cards. It is a young man with white teeth who catches his attention in particular. He is winning. Every time he rakes in the pool, he smiles, almost apologetically. From his vantage point on the floor, the lad regards the young man with admiration; he roots for him silently. The young man wins again and again. But then, watching askance from below, the lad is inattentive for a moment—his gaze must have wandered off—and he sees merely the tail-end of a brief scuffle: The winner and an elder player are standing at their seats; the young man is smiling as the elder drives a knife into his belly. It is this that the master carpenter now remembers so clearly: the look of wonder in his face the moment the young man feels it. The moment he dies. The bareness.

It is only when the master carpenter sees the trader on the square that he can move again. He sees the trader busily loading a cart with goods that are surely meant for sale on Gallows Hill this afternoon. It helps to watch him arrange the apples in such a manner that the bruised and spoiled sides of the fruit are hidden from view, whilst the shiny, color-radiant surfaces are turned to face the potential customers. Only then can he move again.

He hurries off. Work is calling. The master carpenter tries to think about the good price he'll get for the coffin. Even so, he is strangely sad. Strangely spent. He doesn't mean to, but he starts thinking about the dog, that pathetic three-legged cur. He imagines that he takes it home. That he feeds it. He constructs a leg of wood, just for him. And the dog is exceedingly grateful, never to leave his side. He looks down to his side—there—where the dog, perchance, would stand.

One town's many mouths, a chorus fair,
Whilst a head that still doth stare
Rolls to the ground
Without a sound.

Sing a song," suggests the fly.

It is five hours till the boy is to be executed on Gallows Hill, and now he is talking to the fly, which is sitting on his hand.

"A song?" asks the boy. "What kind of song?"

"How about the one, 'where ancient barrows lie between hop and apple orchard'. That one's so mouthwateringly good!"

"I don't know that one. . . ."

"Then recite a poem: 'When the night is still and mild . . .'"

"I don't know that one."

"You're utterly impossible! So tell a story!"

"What kind of story?"

"Just start anywhere!"

"I . . . I can't."

The boy leans back, and the fly takes off. He sees its black body in the light of the cell window. Then it's gone. Perhaps it flew away. It could be sitting on a wall someplace. The boy has an idea:

"Wait!" he says. "I know one!"

He looks about, confused. The hand does not respond. So he just starts telling his tale:

"It must have been four or five years ago. Dad was well—or at least better—and we had a week's work digging up shrubs and roots from a field. It was hard work. The soil was bad. It was more sand than soil. The roots were buried deep, they were tough as rope. The shrubs clawed at our arms till they bled, the sand kept getting in our eyes; we could barely see what we were doing. . . ."

The boy stops. The fly is still in the cell; its black body has just crossed the ray of light from the window. He continues:

"Even so, I was watching a boy playing in

the meadow below. He was playing so carelessly, so recklessly; he'd be no use to anyone back home. He was throwing stones, leaping and hopping in the meadow; he was not a boy who had to work. It was unfair. I envied him. I felt like running him over. Just to stop his games! But there was no time. We were working hard. I wanted to cry. I was tired, I was mad at him. We worked till it got dark, and then I couldn't see whether he was still in the meadow.

"We slept in the farmer's barn. He gave us some food to eat. Dad went to get it for us. He had to shake me awake when he came back.

"'Here,' he said. 'Eat.'

"We ate in silence. Then he told me what he'd heard in the farmyard. That something had happened to the neighbor's daughter. A heap of fieldstones had slid down and buried her.

"'She's dead.'

"She was crushed and suffocated under a pile of stones. We finished our meal in silence. There were bits of meat in the gruel.

"Dad said: 'We should be grateful.'

"'Yes, Dad.'

"Dad checked the straw on the floor and carefully lowered his back to the ground. I could see it in his face.

"'Good night, Niels.'

"'Good night, Dad.'

"I closed my eyes, and I think I fell asleep, but then I suddenly opened my eyes again and sat up. Dad didn't move, but now I understood: That was his sister! The boy in the meadow—*his* sister was dead. He had not been playing in the meadow at all. He just hadn't wanted to go home. He'd have given the world not to think about her being dead.

"I thought about the boy some more. A shiver ran down my spine, as if I'd seen a ghost: Perhaps he didn't dare go home because it was his fault. I saw him standing there: on a pile of stones, arms stretched wide, like a king; his little sister standing down below, looking at him, giggling. . . ."

Niels stopped telling his story. He closed

his eyes, as if trying to remember what came next.

"The next day Dad's back couldn't work anymore, and they didn't want us lying in the barn, so we moved on. . . . End of story."

Someone coughs. Niels can hear a bustle of activity outside. That life is being lived.

His father's back grew steadily worse. The boy recalls the odd memory here and there. He was used to disapproving looks, but now it was his father's bad back that made people stop and stare; now it was the sight of his father that prompted the most furrowed brows. Niels longed desperately for the days when he had been the one—a frail little boy—they looked down on. He had been the object of their scorn; that was easier to bear. Not his dad; he could have sobbed.

One day he came close to knocking a farmer down to the ground, beating him up, for a comment he'd made, so mean. Another day Niels went to fetch some water, and on his way back he passed by two laborers. He could not help but overhear their words.

"There's barely more than a few grains of sand on that old man's spade," said the one.

"Perhaps he should try spading with his back—it's stiff 'nough to dig a ditch with!"

The two men snorted with laughter. The boy forced himself to keep walking.

He handed the water to his father. His father drank.

"Ahh," he said.

The boy turned his back.

"What's the matter?" the father asked.

"I'm not thirsty."

The father could not walk far. He tired quickly. And he was sick. He threw up on the roadside. The boy stood and watched: He was so thin, his back so bent. He looked like a sheet of paper folded in half.

The boy supported his father. He provided food. But he felt it to the bone when his father gripped his arm. His hoarse voice:

"We will not steal!" he said. "No matter what: We won't do it!"

The boy shook his head. Motioned with his head again. Then he said: "No, Dad."

His father loosened his grip.

"And remember: You're going home to your oven."

Always this fear of the workhouse. It rooted in the boy; the sight of a uniform sent him running.

The boy never stole. He collected apples. Apples that would have rotted on the ground. And he played games. Boys' games. He practiced throwing. With stones. One, two, three stones. One of the stones veered off course and hit the branch of an apple tree. The boy collected only those apples that had fallen to the ground. Then he took them to his father. No America.

Niels remembers one day his father could not get his back up off the floor. He lay in a shed, a hand under his back and a bottle in the crook of his arm. The boy was desperate. He talked about his mother. If only she had lived.

"Imagine Mum hadn't been ill," he said.

"There's no point, Niels."

"Yes, but wouldn't that have been good?"

"Forget it."

"No. Wouldn't it?"

"I don't know."

"No, but I do."

The father took a sip from the bottle without looking at the boy.

"Don't you ever think about her?" asked the boy.

"No," answered the father.

"I do. All the time."

"Don't."

"I can't."

"You have to."

The last words came out hard. They both fell silent. Then the boy said:

"It's not your fault, Dad."

"It's nobody's fault," he said.

"Then you do think about her!" he cried.

The father did not answer, just closed his eyes. He looked as if just moving his eyelids hurt.

The fly is back on the hand. Silent. Through the window the boy can see a cut of bleak blue sky.

He can see the road ahead, there, where he met the girl.

He was sitting in the middle of a field. His father's back was bad. They had found a place to rest under a clump of trees. There he lay. Niels sat in the field.

There was a boy like a statue in a field.

He had not said so out loud, but that's what he was doing once more: waiting for the one who would not come.

"Ha!" was all the girl said.

He had not heard her come. The sun blinded his eyes. He had to shield them with his hand.

"The scarecrow moves!" she laughed.

Niels got to his feet.

"This is our field," he said.

"Is that so?" the girl answered. "And I'm carrying this basket for the sake of it."

"Aren't you too busy to stand here talking to me?" he asked.

"I've been told to watch out for beggars!"

Her cheeks were red. He wanted to say something really smart, but when he opened his mouth, nothing came out.

"You're the worst beggar I've ever met," she said.

"My father is very sick," he said. "I think he's going to die."

Even Niels was surprised. The last bit he hadn't meant to say out loud. The girl watched him closely.

"Where do you live?"

He was about to lie, rattle off his lines, but he just shrugged instead. The girl shifted the basket from one hip to the other. Then she pointed to a meadow between a stretch of forest and a field.

"Tonight," she said, and left.

Niels was there, in the meadow, before the

sun went down. He waited. Before him there was a path that split in two. Finally, he saw her coming down one of them. He waved. She did not wave back. She was carrying a bowl of soup.

"Thank you," he said.

"Do you have your father's eyes?"

"No. My mother's."

"Is she sick too?"

"No, she's fine," he said.

"Tomorrow night," she said, turned, and left.

The boy hears the warden locking someone into the prison. He cannot hear any talk, only steps on the stones. He feels a brush of hope before it disappears, and a family is standing by the cell. They're staring at him. Their faces are red, their boots are wet. *There must still be snowdrifts outside*, thinks the boy.

It is only once the mother spits.

The brother says: *You child murderer!*

The sister hisses: *We will be standing in the first row to see the blood gush from your neck!*

That he understands: This is the boy's family.

They damn him to Hell, and they keep on damning him. Outside, the dog begins to bark; perhaps it's afraid they'll hurt him. But it doesn't matter. They have every right to call him whatever they please. Damn him to wherever they please.

He cannot hear the dog anymore. Perhaps someone chased it away. But now he cannot hear the family, either. He looks down at his arms: no, he hasn't blocked his ears with hands—cannot do so with the one hand anyway. He can feel his head about to burst. Words and sounds twist and turn, become a growling gruel, the rustle of thousands of nails against his skull. They plunge down his throat in a cold clamor; they stay embedded there. He cannot breathe. Red-black dots are dancing before his eyes.

Now I'm going to die, thinks the boy.

But then the howling mass combines into a regular sound, a row of words, like a song, and his gaze rests on the mother's face. It is still red,

distorted by hate and pain, the spray of spit
before her mouth, but the words that emerge
are like a verse, a poem:

> When the night is still and mild
> And all things quiet through,
> My son, my dearest little child!
> Then I shall come to you.

> For God has granted me,
> When sleep comes over thee,
> Now and then
> In a dream with you to be.

> I see you draw, write,
> Read your book so carefully;
> You learn to be bright,
> Pious, and clever for me.

> Your cheeks are red,
> Your eyes are blue,
> Those sweet lips in your bed
> I oft did kiss for you.

Pray, do you think of her
Who mourns her only son?
Pray, does she recur
When evening prayers are done?

Pray, do you remember my call?
Pray, do you remember my face?
Oh, can you forget that hour at all
You left my sweet embrace?

In the forest like a lonesome bird
Only to sing sorrow's song,
Ever mournful and unheard,
Of you my thoughts prolong.

Oh, if you knew my yearning,
You'd make all haste,
And flee your prison burning,
To her who loves you most.

To her who bore you here
In woe and fear,

Who christened you in tears—
And loves you ever dear!

Farewell, farewell, my darling!
Softly I sigh your name;
Never to think away my yearning,
Your loss never to reclaim.

I close my hands and tend
To you, my son of sorrow!
Each hour to God I send,
To you, my heartfelt prayer!

The boy only shifts his gaze from the mother's
lips when the family turns and leaves.

There are four hours till the boy is to be executed on Gallows Hill, and the mayor is sitting at his desk fiddling with a wooden figurine. This is nearly too much to bear: the way they keep pestering him!

One meeting after another. He spent God knows how many hours with the Bakers' Guild, which is up in arms about falling bread prices. They claim to be in the direst of straits, they want to raise their prices, but what would have happened if he'd let them? Then the poor folk would've been up in arms.

The mayor feels as if he's buried in complaints: Townsfolk complaining about the begging on the streets—shall he drag them to the work-house himself!? Townsfolk complaining about the leaking gutters—shall he go and clean them himself!? Townsfolk wanting to know what he's doing about the threat of cholera—can he, single-handedly, ward off an epidemic at the city gates?! Townsfolk complaining about the seepage from pig farms that freezes over-night and turns the streets into a skating rink. Choice example: He sent some men to break up the ice—but the tenants didn't want to pay for it!

The mayor hammers the figurine into the desk, and now he takes a good, long look at it. It was standing on his desk when he took up his post. It's carved into the shape of a fat mon-key. Of course the thought crossed his mind that it was meant to be a spiteful model of him. But he likes it. And who says the *town* isn't a fat-bellied monkey—wanting bananas stuck in both hands!

The mayor feels as if he is being pushed and pulled from all sides. That folk keep trying to get money—bananas—out of his pockets. And they won't stop till they've torn the clothes from his body. Nobody will be happy, it seems, till he's standing on the square stark naked!

The image of him standing naked in the middle of the town square reminds the mayor of something else: the lad who will be executed on Gallows Hill later that day. His mood improves at once. He leans back in his chair and lists three undeniably good things about executions.

One: Executions prove that the mayor is a man of action—that will serve him well for a long time to come!

Two: Folk won't have time to file any more complaints today—they'll all be up on Gallows Hill!

Three: A man can't say it, but a brawling monkey can—that's *one* problem less!

The problem calls for radical means. He's quite clear about that. The mayor has thought about building higher walls around the city, building a regular city wall. This would be an effective way of keeping the beggars out—especially all those peasant children—who are such a blemish on the town.

A city wall, perhaps more executions. Surely a dumb wooden monkey is entitled to ask: Wouldn't the elimination of the poor eliminate poverty? A wretched, deranged murderer of a boy—like the one to be executed today—doesn't have a life worth living. Wouldn't it be in everyone's best interests? Wouldn't the death of one of his kind improve the lives of the rest of us? Isn't this proof enough of the common good?

The mayor starts at the knock at the door. *Who could that be now?! Hardly likely His Royal Highness, the king, here to pin the Medal of Honor to his chest!*

"Come in!"

A large man in filthy clothing is standing in the doorway. This does not bode well.

"Stengel, from Odense," the man presents himself.

It may as well be Stengel from America! thinks the mayor. As if he didn't have enough towns-folk to take care of. The world is standing at his door, hat in hand.

"Yes?"

"It is me," says the large man. "Me . . . the exe-cutioner."

Now the mayor looks him over carefully. Does the face of a man reveal that he executes men for a living? All the mayor can see is how mild tempered the man is.

"I need to check the scaffold, Mr. Mayor," he says. "But I'm looking for an assistant."

"An assistant?"

The executioner clears his throat.

"Someone to hold the head, Mr. Mayor."

Me! is the mayor's first thought. *He wants* me *to do it!* Then he thinks: *Nonsense! Pull yourself together. Defer him to the chief inspector—let him figure out the rest.* The mayor defers to the chief inspector, and bids him farewell.

"Good-bye, Mr. Mayor."

The man nods in parting.

"How do you do it!?"

The mayor is no less surprised than the executioner. He has no idea why he asks. Why doesn't he just let the man close the door, so he can have some peace?

"Err . . . with an ax, sir," says the executioner. "I bought it from my predecessor. First-class quality."

"Yes, but how do you *do* it?"

There is a moment of silence. The executioner shifts his weight.

"The ax is exactly as it should be: heavy, but not too hard to handle," he explains. "It demands your full attention at the start of the swing, but then it takes over; it cuts like a scythe through a blade of grass. It's a part of me, yet stands apart—like a son. . . ."

But all at once the executioner clams up, looks down at the ground in shame. The mayor is at a loss for words, but feels he ought to take charge. Be pragmatic. Be mayor.

"And what are you thinking of spending your wage on, sir?" the mayor asks.

"On food," the executioner answers.

The mayor gives him a nod. He is already staring down at the papers in front of him.

"And I'm saving up for a little dinghy I've got my eye on, Mr. Mayor," concludes the executioner.

The mayor winces, ducks his head even farther, and dismisses the executioner with a wave of the hand. The mayor doesn't look up.

"Good-bye, then, Mr. Mayor."

Once he hears the door click shut, the mayor leans back in his chair. He stays sitting like this for a long time.

He thinks how easy it would be. He could get up, pack his clothes, walk to the harbor, and set sail on the first available ship!

He rests a hand on the wooden figurine, as if it were the mast of a boat. The whole time he had thought the monkey was staring ahead in blind fury, indeed *was* blind, or perhaps the artist had simply forgotten to do the eyes. Now he thinks the monkey's eyes are cast down, staring at its own navel.

The mayor thinks about the time he was a boy, when he used to play in the hills beyond the town. There was something special about the clouds: the way they darted across the heavens in a gray-white belt, the blue behind, the green landscape in the foreground, and the yellow fields—as if layer upon layer had been stacked in a certain way. He used to love standing with his arms hanging down by his sides; he liked to think he was a landmark in that patch of the world.

Again he thinks: *Get up and go.*

Just like that.

And meet the world.

One town's many mouths, a chorus fair,
Whilst a head that still doth stare
Rolls to the ground
Without a sound.

It is past noon, the sun slants down over the town roofs, and there are three hours till the boy is to be executed on Gallows Hill. He looks up to the sun.

"Am I a bad person?" he asks.

The boy cannot tell how much time passes without an answer, but he can see the sun has moved.

He's been watching it. The sun—or that patch it makes on the floor. He has tried to hold on to, take note of, its slightest move. He cannot remember shifting his gaze, but the light has moved. A great deal, in fact. Can't we just hold on?

The boy thinks that sometimes it's just *too*

late. No longer possible. One moment it is, and the next, it isn't. That's how it feels, anyway.

He is thinking about his father. About how his father was, when their life was good. His father worked for two men; once, his big hands lifted a stone that everyone else in the field had given a wide berth. Back then his father bore him over sticks and stones, but all the while the boy felt as if he were the one who was in charge.

Then the father's body was broken. The boy thinks about one of those days when his father had to sit by the road and rest. They had been sitting there for some time:

"Are you feeling better?" asked the boy.

"No."

The boy was about to ask again, but his father was holding tight to the boy's leg, just above the knee. There was still vigor in those blue-red fingers.

"Ouch."

"Sorry," said the father.

"It doesn't matter."

"I'm sorry."

They sat looking down over the town. *There are fields, and there is the town,* the boy thought. *Someone has made this country road, many have walked along this way, and many will walk this way again.* Perhaps this was how the boy tried to understand it. That it was too late.

Near the end, the father was so thin it looked like you could stick a hand right through him. The boy carried their mean possessions. Even so, the father had to rest several times. They took whatever came their way. They chewed on whatever took the worst of the hunger.

The father sat down. They were sitting by the roadside. Usually they waded into a field, hiding under cover. Many people passed, either in horse carts or on foot. The father never looked up.

There had to be an end to this. The boy just didn't want to see it. He watched the father's face. The pain there became steadily worse.

"Does it hurt really bad?"

"No," said the father.

"Yes it does," said the boy.

"No, not at all," answered the father. "I'll try to get up."

The boy looked at him. The father asked:

"But it won't work, will it?"

The father sat bent forward, a grimace on his face.

"Let me help you," said the boy.

"That's just what I thought!" said the father with a short laugh.

"Let me help."

"No. It's about you now."

The boy wanted to pull him up, but the father shook his head.

"No, my boy."

Then they noticed a uniformed man approaching them. A policeman. Perhaps someone had called him, perhaps it was just a coincidence. Niels remembers his shiny black polished shoes.

"Go!" said the father.

"Come!" said the boy. "I'll get you up!"

The father removed the boy's hand from his arm.

"You go along your way now," he said.

"But, Dad . . ."

"Do as I say, Niels!"

The father gave him a shove that knocked him off his feet. But the boy was instantly up again. He looked in the direction of the policeman, then back at his father. The father did not look up.

Then the boy ran. Ran for all he was worth. Without looking back.

Ran till he was far out of town.

Now the boy can hear the dog bark. It's a different kind of bark, as if the dog has seen someone it knows or really likes. It's such a nutter of a three-legged dog. He wishes he could stroke it.

He can see it now. The sun has shifted on the floor again.

He thinks about the girl. That he ran in that direction.

On the second day he slept in a dike with a view of a little house. He daren't go closer. He just lay there, staring at the house. You could hardly call it a farm. It was just a hut with a stable joined to it. But he dreamt the house was his. That it was theirs. He had built it for them. She watched from below and waved, one hand resting on her hip; he could see she was pregnant.

Three days later and he was back. In the meadow with the forked path, where he'd last seen her. He had wanted to say good-bye, but she had kissed him. She had grabbed hold of the hair at the nape of his neck with one hand, as if she'd wanted to smack him in the face with the other. But then she had let go, turned round, and disappeared down a fork in the path.

Now that he was back, he could feel the longing for her in every part of his body. He slept in the meadow, and during the day he ran up to the road and back again, in the hope of seeing her. He daren't go too far for food. It was cold and gusty. Dust particles tore at his eyes; folk remained indoors.

When she did come walking up the path, he stayed on the ground where he was. He could not believe it. But it was her. She stopped walking when he got up. She was carrying a basket, which she put down. She stood a couple of yards behind the basket; he, the same distance away, as if this were a child's game they were about to play.

"Hi," he said.

"There is food in the basket," she answered.

"For whom?"

"Perhaps I'll meet a nice boy out here."

It sounded all wrong. She didn't look at him when she said it. She looked up over the meadow.

"I'm happy to see you again."

"Where is your father?" she asked.

"My mother died when I was born," he said.

She looked in his eyes for the first time. *Should she be looking at me like that?* he thought as they sat down.

"Eat," she said.

"How could you know I'd be here?"

"We don't know anything."

"You do."

"No, I don't tell the truth."

But then she touched her hair, tousled it in that special way: quick, quick, slow.

They stayed sitting there till the sun disappeared. She should have been back on the farm long ago.

"I had a dream about you," he said.

"When was the last time you ate?" she asked.

"I had a dream about you."

"Don't do that," she said. "Eat some more."

"I built a farm."

"I don't want to hear any more."

"You were pregnant."

"Niels. Stop."

"Okay. So close your eyes."

"They are closed."

"Then make as if you've closed them."

"Eat now."

"Do it."

"Yes."

"Now."

"Fast or slow?"

"Slowly."

"Okay."

"Now we are in America."

This time he kissed her.

"So why did you leave her?"

It is the fly asking—perhaps in response to a mutter from the hand. The boy stares from the one to the other, still keeping tabs on the light on the floor from the corner of his eye. He feels the dizziness, the sweat like a river between his shoulder blades.

What a strange friendship this is, he thinks. *Between a swollen, humming hand and a tiny, loudmouthed fly.* The world is the meeting place of the strange.

"Don't try to weasel out of it now!" rasps the fly. "Why?"

"Because she made it impossible for me to lie," answered the boy.

He saw her, and only her, when she came down the path again. She came whenever she could get away. When she finally did come, he jumped up to meet her and immediately started talking about the farm in America. But he got the feeling she didn't want to hear it.

"Stop it now," she said.

He went on. She tried to stop him.

"Can't we just sit here together?"

He nodded. And he meant it.

"Smile," she said.

He tried. It became a grimace. Because he wanted to talk about the future instead.

One day she brought along a baked omelet. It tasted heavenly.

"You must make an omelet like that for our child's birthday," he said. "We'll lay a table in the yard."

She shook her head, rested a cheek against his shoulder.

"It doesn't matter," she said.

Now he can see that he was the one who needed convincing. It was *he* who still needed to see the farm. Not her. For every time he saw her, he knew it was a lie. That he would never build a farm for her. That he was never going to America. That there was only one thing destined for him: Sooner or later he would end up in the workhouse.

So he kept talking. One day she cut him off. She stood up. He could see the tears in her eyes.

"Can't you see what you mean to me?"

"Yes, but the stable is going to be—"

"No, Niels. If you had the slightest idea what I feel for you, you wouldn't say another word."

A tear slipped down her cheekbone. She turned, and left. He remained sitting where he was, staring at his hands, till it became too dark to tell the one from the other.

"One day when I was waiting for her, I looked down at my hands," he recalls. "I mean, really looked at them. And then I understood. That it was already too late."

His mind continued on this track, but he did not want to think at all.

So he hid. He could see her sitting there, where they liked to sit. He could see her fussing with her hair. He could see her looking out for him. Heard her call. But he stayed hidden. He did not answer. He waited till she could wait no more. Till she had to go back to her work on the farm. Then he jumped up. He went to the spot where her body had flattened the grass.

"Why did you hide?"

It was Niels who asked, Niels who replied.

"I guess I don't believe.

"What don't you believe?

"Me." Then he walked the other way. To the forest.

Just as he came out on the other side, he saw the dog. The boy looked around for a weapon. But it just stood there. As if it had been waiting for him. Then he noticed it was missing a leg. When he walked on, the dog limped after him. He tried to get rid of it. He was afraid it was vicious. But every time he turned, the dog was there. Incredible how fast it could move on just three legs. Then he waited.

Thereafter they were inseparable. It followed

him everywhere. They ate together. Slept tucked
up close together. For weeks. Months.

Also that night in the barn. It was very cold,
the ground was frozen, there was ice on the
beams above. It was difficult for the boy to
unclench his hands. So he made a fire.

Just a small one, he thought. *Just till we warm
up a little.*

He could feel the warmth of a body bigger
than a dog's. From a woman . . .

It was the dog that woke him. Sparks must
have flown several meters, landing on the pile
of old horse blankets. The barn was on fire.
Flames licked up the rear wall. They were
already so big. There was no way to stop them.
If you came anywhere near, your eyes and face
burnt. It was impossible to breathe.

PUUUFF! And the fire licked up into the
roof. The boy and the dog slipped out, just as
the rear of the barn collapsed, sending a million
myriad embers into a black sky. The boy stared
in horror at these powers destroying a barn
in no time at all. He thought about the river.

Mississippi. If only the river ran *here*—with all that water—perhaps something could have been done! Perhaps the flames could have been stopped. But now it was hopeless. The boy stayed standing where he was. He remained standing, did nothing, till he felt a heavy hand on his shoulder.

The boy hears the warden talking to someone. A door being opened and closed.

He looks at the fly, at the hand, at the fly again. At a patch of sun on the floor.

That's odd, he thinks. *The moment you let go of the stone, it's too late to change your mind. But if you don't say or do something, it is also too late.*

And so it was. Both the one way and the other. He should not have let go, and he should have said it.

He could have put down the stone and said to that little boy:

"I'm going to America."

The sun feels almost warm; it makes the cobblestones shine wet and black. There are two hours till the boy is to be executed on Gallows Hill, and the priest, standing at the church door, has always felt it so fitting for a church to face the prison door.

He is thinking about one of his parishioners, a woman who came by and said if it had been *her* child that knave had murdered, she'd have clawed his eyes out herself.

The priest looks at the prison. Could the devil's finest work be hidden behind those walls?

He steps over the cobblestones, calmly picking his way through little islands of gritty snow and ice. He raps his knuckles rhythmically on the door, for just as he told that woman this morning, God will be the ultimate bond between offender and justice, for sure.

The warden opens the door. His mouth is full of food. The priest makes no comment, but the warden cuts a guilty glance at the baked omelet and bread that are lying on the table.

"A girl came by with it," he explains. "But I thought the lad won't get much use out of it, now that he's going to be . . ."

The warden jerks his head sideways, red in the face, his beard clotted with bits of food, but the priest just motions toward the cell, so the warden walks ahead to open the door.

The boy is sitting on the bed. How can such a little body harbor so much evil? The priest stops to think for a moment. Should he be intimidated? Should he be afraid?

The priest is not afraid. He sits down next to the boy and asks whether they should fold their hands in prayer. The boy shakes his head. The priest looks down at one of the boy's hands and understands: the boy cannot fold his hands. So he asks if he should pray for them both. The boy does not answer.

The priest prays. He talks about sin and punishment. And forgiveness.

Then he talks about the boy's offense. Gives the deed its proper name. The priest cannot glean any response from the boy. Perhaps the boy is dim-witted.

"Haven't you been to church before?" asks the priest.

The boy shakes his head.

"Ever?"

"Not as far as I can remember . . ."

The boy is not dim. That much the priest can see. He is scheming. Stalling. But the priest is ready. He asks:

"And why not?"

The priest braces himself, thinks, *Now the hour of evil is come; now it comes like fire.*

"We were chased away," replies the boy.

"From church?"

"From every place there was life."

"Why?" The priest is still wary.

"They probably thought we had come to beg."

The priest was expecting a vicious, full-frontal attack. Perhaps it will sneak up from behind—a calculated ambush?

"Who is 'we'?" he asks.

"My father."

"Your father," says the priest. "And where is your father now?"

"He's dead."

The priest sees the distortion in an otherwise expressionless face. He feels a brush of doubt. Till he understands. *'Tis for my sake. Now God is testing me!* The priest chooses his words carefully.

"And you didn't come to beg?" he asks.

The figure on the bed shakes its head.

"Then why did you come?" asks the priest.

The boy opens his mouth but does not answer. Then he shakes his head. He mumbles:

"I don't know."

"Excuse me?"

"I don't know," repeats the boy.

"No," says the priest. "But do you know why I'm here now?"

The boy shrugs his shoulders, and the priest lays a hand on one of them. "'Whoever does not receive the kingdom of God like a child will never enter it. . . .'"

"But I am not a boy."

"What are you, then?" asks the priest, expecting the worst. He can feel a shiver run up his arm, and he looks down at the boy's deformed and discolored hand. Is evil forcing its way out?

"I don't know," he answers. "I just want to be me."

"Perhaps ultimately there is only one who can know for sure. . . ."

You are a lamb, thinks the priest compassionately. *A sick, three-legged little lamb.*

On and on, over and again, the priest tries to get the boy to surrender. To confess. Repent. Break down. The priest holds on, but the soul of this boy will be neither poked nor pierced. *Is it because I can't reach him?* he thinks. *Is this evil in distilled form? Or have I got him after all? Is silence the only defense against God Almighty?* But by and by the priest thinks: *I don't know who he is. He is neither boy nor man. What is he?*

Finally the priest gets up to go. Is this a victory? Half a victory?

The priest is nearly out the door when it comes.

"That story about the paralyzed man . . . ," says the boy.

"When the Son of God, Jesus, heals the paralyzed man?"

The boy nods. The priest smiles. He will welcome the boy to the fold.

"Luke, chapter five, verses twelve to twenty-six," he says.

The boy does not answer.

The priest opens the Bible and reads. He reads about Jesus healing the leper, about how this attracts crowds from far and wide—from Galilee, Judaea, and Jerusalem. They want Jesus to cure all sorts of diseases.

Some men arrive with a paralyzed man on a bed, but there are too many people crowding round Jesus, so they cannot get to him. But they crawl up onto the roof, remove some tiles, and lower the paralyzed man down into the crowd in front of him. Jesus tells the paralyzed man to get up, take his bed, and go home—which he does at once. The people have seen miracles—they believe Jesus to be the true Son of God!

The boy has listened. The boy has nodded. Now is the time.

"Are you ready to surrender to God?" asks the priest.

The boy is silent for a moment. *Now he'll fall,* thinks the priest. *Now he'll fall into God's embrace.*

"Those men . . . ," the boy says.

"The disciples?" asks the priest.

"No. The men."

"Which *men?*"

"The men who lowered the paralyzed man down into the crowd," says the boy. "What were their names?"

"What were they *called?* . . . I don't know . . . but it's not about *them!*"

The boy is silent. The priest feels a fly near his ear.

"It's a story about *faith*," he explains.

"If they hadn't held on, the paralyzed man would never have gotten in," says the boy. "They helped him. Were there four of them?"

"I . . . I don't know," says the priest. "It just says 'some men.' It's the miracle you need to think about. That someone, who could not walk, all at once gets up and goes home."

"One man at each end would hold it steady," the boy explains. "Just four men would do."

"What is it with you and those men?!" the priest exclaims.

The boy looks down at his hands. The ruined one and the other one. The priest needs to listen very closely to hear what he mumbles. But he hears it.

The boy says:

"Perhaps the men could also pull the bed *up.*"

≣ ⪤

The priest is standing in the prison door, facing the church, and now he can feel it, his exhaustion. The sweat under his gown.

He can't quite decide how he feels.

He tries thinking about his sermon for Sunday. After an execution the church will be full. They will be there, all of them, and *they* will surrender. Perhaps that is why God has sent this lad. *He* will not find God, but the others will. The priest casts a fitting phrase, takes a moment to savor the words: "A drop of evil transformed to an ocean of goodness."

But the words please his palate only for a moment. Now he realizes what misguided vanity it all has been, how his mind had tried to dodge down an even path. He bows his head, feels the gush of shame.

Now he is loath to admit that everything still revolves around the one who is sitting in the cell. The priest has simply underestimated his task. He has acted over-eagerly, was too focused on victory, too sure of a conquest. He has mistaken success for truth. He knows that his parishioners see the flock only when he makes an example of another standing beyond it. This is the shortest route to success. But truth does not concern him or them alone. It's about being part of the flock.

He realizes that this wasn't the decisive—just the preemptive—battle. And the next will be fought on Gallows Hill. It comes to him so cleanly, so effortlessly, he hardly dares to think the thought: *It is here one can work with eternities!*

When the lad is forced to his knees, the priest will be there. When the boy looks up from the scaffold, the priest will be ready. He will be the recognizable face in the crowd; something to cling on to in his final hour.

The priest will not bide the other ninety-nine lambs. Just heed the one leaving the flock on the scaffold. He will search every bush, every shrub, till he finds it and takes it in his arms. A sick, three-legged little lamb.

Every member of the flock must be gathered

together. Their number must be complete. There is only one thing that counts: When the ax falls, there must be one hundred out of one hundred!

> One town's many mouths, a chorus fair,
> Whilst a head that still doth stare
> Rolls to the ground
> Without a sound.

There is one hour till the boy is to be executed on Gallows Hill, and the warden brings him half a loaf of bread. The boy can smell the scent of some other food cloying to his clothing, but the warden says nothing, and the boy does not ask.

The boy knows nobody listens.

He tried to tell the judge and those other men that he did not set fire to the barn on purpose. He lit the fire because he was very cold. But they did not listen. He was arrested for burning down the barn intentionally. As well as two other buildings: a stable and another barn someplace he had never heard of. Then he was led away.

The boy leaves the bread lying on the floor. It smells freshly baked. The fly lands on the bread, and the boy lets it be.

"Help yourself."

The fly crawls over the bread silently, as if it were looking for the best place to start. It stops where the bread is broken.

"How do I know when you're full?" asks the boy. "When you fly away?"

The fly does not answer.

The patch of sun is approaching that point where floor becomes a wall. *Is it the light or my sight that is blurring?* thinks the boy.

After the boy was sentenced for arson, he was put to work splitting stones in the yard. It was hard work, many hours a day.

The sheriff's son came out and watched him in the yard whilst he worked. The sheriff's son was well dressed, his staring eyes level below the neatly combed hair. He was not tall, could not have been very old, but spoke as if he were much older. The little boy spit on the ground every time he spoke.

"You take forever!" he said, spitting, as if it were his job to ensure that the boy kept his nose to the grindstone.

"Mind your own business," the boy said, and kept working.

"It's for your own good," the little boy replied crossly, "or it will all end very badly for you!"

The boy did not answer, he bent over his stones instead.

"Or else you'll end up in the workhouse!"

He tried to block his ears. He tried to drown out the little boy's talk by hammering and hammering on the stones. But still he could hear them so clearly. Each and every word.

"JUST LIKE YOUR FATHER!!!"

The boy's body jerked upright.

"Who says so?" The boy narrowed his eyes.

The sheriff's son laughed maliciously, spat. "Because that's where people in your family always end up!" he yelled. "Including you! That is, unless you get your head chopped off first!"

The boy turned his back on the yelling lad; if he could have, he would have turned his back on himself.

The boy can see that the patch of sun has inched up the first bit of the wall. He can feel his body shaking, whether due to the fever or something else. Even so, the fly is back on the hand. Now it is the fly that whispers, the fly that says:

"Yep, he left his dad in the workhouse."

It says this as if it were attending a tea party with the hand. Perhaps this is why he nods. Why Niels wants to tell the story himself. This is true: His father is in the workhouse. Unless he's dead now.

The boy stayed near town for several weeks. He left the dog in an old shed with a little food and water. He was scared out of his wits as he circled that place he knew as hell on Earth. One day he dared to go in. In to the people with the black-coin eyes. He posed as a town messenger ordered to collect blankets from the mite-infested loft. But the boy only got as far as the door. Not that anyone tried to stop him, he couldn't bring himself to take another step; he had seen too much.

He saw his father in profile in the far corner. He was sitting bent close to the wall, as if something written there would take the rest of his life to decipher. Hollowed cheeks, eyes dug deep into their sockets, impossibly thin; skin and sinew ready to slip off the bones, onto the floor. The boy could not move. He turned and went on his way before his father could see him.

Every night in prison, Niels dreamt about people with black coins in their heads. Sometimes, they were unknown masses, lumbering toward him; sometimes it was his father, sitting on a chair, staring at him. Every day he split stones, and every day the sheriff's son came out into the yard; the son loomed larger and larger in the boy's mind with every word spoken, every insult, the spitting.

"Someone like you will never have a real life!"

He tried to ignore him. He thought he succeeded. But he didn't.

The little boy lounged against the wall with his hands in his pockets, like a regular lout.

"Someone like you is just a burden!"

The boy did not reply. He hammered into a stone, which split into four.

"Your family is a stone round the town's neck!"

The boy could feel his whole body shaking.

"That's not true," he mumbled. "You did good, Dad."

The sheriff's son spat on the ground.

"And your mother is Mad Martina!" he called.

The sheriff's son did not realize he had hit the spot. He was too busy spitting and thinking of something else to say. He took no notice of the effect his words had on the boy.

The boy had never known his mother. He only knew she had black hair. Once, he had seen a picture of a woman and a child someplace, and he had imagined his mother to be someone like that. But he knew Mad Martina.

He had seen her at the workhouse. That time he went to see his father. She was sitting in a window up in the loft. She called to him when he came, and called to him when he left. The boy looked up as he walked away. In that instant she lifted her skirts to expose her crotch.

The boy had stopped cutting stones, but by the time the sheriff's son realized how much he had riled the boy, it was too late. Niels had lifted the stone. The sheriff's little boy swallowed his spit and ran. Niels aimed for the blond head, and threw. The stone struck with a speed and precision that surprised him. As if he had skimmed the water with the perfect pitch, which sent the stone flying from one riverbank to the other. The sheriff's son was thrown to the ground at once. After a long moment the blood seeped out of the back of his head and colored the hair and yard dark.

For some reason, in that very instant he remembered where he had seen that picture of mother and child: One night he had stood looking into the window of a house. The lights were on, but the living room was empty. The family must have been in another room, but there it was, the picture, as if the lights were lit for its sake alone. For the sake of mother and child.

The boy cannot remember any more. Other than being beaten. Hard. Thrown onto a floor. Dragged away, and sentenced for murder. He never said a word to the judge or the other men.

The boy is keeping an eye on the fly, which is back on the bread.

"Do you fly because you've decided to fly?" he asks. "Or because you got a fright?"

The fly trips over the hand. *That's odd*, the boy thinks. It stays mum whenever he asks a question, but at all other times it never hesitates to speak its mind.

"Or do you just fly?"

He doesn't want to think about the girl but he thinks of her now. About that day a fly landed on her lip, again and again. That day they tossed burs at each other. That day they ended up kissing each other, again and again. He thinks of her sitting in the field. How she tousled and fixed her hair afterward. In that way she always did: quick, quick, slow.

Now the fly has landed on the hand again. It is up to something, trippling back and forth on the hand. It stops in midstep. Moves again, edges out onto the tip of what used to be a thumb. A good place to shout from. Then it declares:

"Now the boy will die!"

The hand does not answer. It doesn't twitch a muscle.

"Perhaps one of you would like to whistle a tune?"

No one answers.

"Okay," says the fly. "If that's the way you want to play it."

It rubs its hind legs together.

"That calls for a showdown!" it shouts. "Rock, paper, or scissors!"

And then it laughs. That's how it sounds.

Like a bubbly laugh. He does not know why, but the boy smiles.

Then the fly takes off. It is lost to the eye against the dark walls, but twice it crosses the light ray—it seems to loop—before flying out the window. The boy is sure: He sees it duck through the rails and fly up into the sky, before he is blinded by the light. The fly is gone.

The boy gathers up the bread. It is surprisingly warm. But then he realizes the bread is not warm; his hand is too cold.

The boy sits motionlessly for a long time. He studies the bread carefully. It has a hard crust, brown on top and lighter down along the sides. The near-white grains in the bread, a few oval pockets of air. For a moment he thinks about the master baker or the apprentice, who must have baked it.

The boy tries to gauge if he's hungry. No, he doesn't think he is. But what else could this feeling be?

The boy moves over to the window. Here he pushes the bread through the bars. He is dizzy, grips the iron rails. He hopes to hear the dog bark, but hears nothing. He calls, but there is no answer. Perhaps someone has chased it away? Perhaps it has gone along its way? Animals have a sense telling them something is about to happen. It knows he will die soon. Perhaps it is already looking for a new companion?

Then the boy hears a door being opened in the building. He hears talking, without being able to discern the words. But he can hear more than one person. Steps on the stones. Many steps. Perhaps five or six men. They are coming closer. The men.

All at once his limbs feel tired, but he is very much awake.

"Now they are coming," the boy says to himself.

There is no point in sitting down. This, too, he says to himself.

He is ready.

The sky bears the same blue as the eyes of innocence; the sun is shining like the well-dressed deputy of God on this winter's afternoon, beckoning with the promise of early spring—'tis on its way, 'tis on its way—and now the boy is to be executed on Gallows Hill!

The poet has arrived early, so he can stand in the front row. He is scribbling busily in his book. He towers over most of the crowd, a little unsure on his legs, as if he were an over-grown child looking for his mum. But he is reeling on his heels to take it all in. He sucks in impressions and images like marmalade pulls in flies.

The poet twists his body, absorbs his surroundings, and bows his head. Then he buries his nose in his pages, filling them with wave after wave of painted words. The poet writes:

The little children cannot be still; they snap up expectations and vibrations, as if we were attending a feast! As if royalty were expected. The entire town seems to be assembled here! Even a man-hating rat would feel lonesome in town today— "Bah! I'll have to find another town to skulk in today!!"

But is the execution the most important thing of all? Not necessarily so. People are many-sided beings. Folk turn to look in every possible and impossible way, with an eye for a pretty lass, a choice remark, a thrifty trade, or a quick fight. A swarm of birds, like a pointed arrow headed for milder skies, would think: "What is the entire town doing down there? I cannot make head nor tail of this crowd. That these beings should be the creators of grand buildings and lofty poetry is absurd. In an anthill there is order in chaos, but

that down there is sheer madness! Head
south, dear friends, head south!"

The poet puts the notebook in his pocket, only to fish it up again immediately. His eyes are on stalks, yet buried in his head. He sees everything, feels everything. And writes. He stares, rakes it all in, and yet tunes ever inward: He is the metronome. The real music is composed by seismic interactions of the organs in his body. Is the heart hammering harder? Are the lungs keeping pace? Does the stomach contract? Does it hurt down below? What say you, blood? Does the liver object?

He draws out to the right and finds a little mound to perch on. He is swept up by his scribbles; they fill the page with words, like children crowding in, covering the ground of Gallows Hill.

The poet sees, absorbs, and writes:

No man could falter on Gallows Hill
today—not for lack of food and drink. Bread
is on sale, and one particularly perilous

temptation—raisin bread—is selling well.
Ouch! And everything can be washed down
with a drink, especially amidst the ale
club of males, as you could call those men
gathered around the well-stocked innkeeper,
who is making sure you can find warmth in
a brandy or a good, strong beer. Here the
mood has been jolly for a good while; folk
are happily falling in sync with a person
they possibly know.

A flock of children are engaged in a
game so vicious it makes your head spin
and your stomach churn: Call it a game one
more time! Like Roman gladiators of former
times, they seem to rip at one another
savagely; to the eye of the observer, a
genuine flensing of flesh, but for the zeal
with which they fling themselves into the
midst of their playmates. Threaded into one
another like many-limbed monsters, they
pull, tear, and claw away. That legs and
arms don't snap like pencils is a mystery.
A single bloody nose (apart from red ears)
is the only visible sign of injury. That they
are obviously enjoying themselves—despite
scornful, devilish laughter—is beyond all
comprehension.

The children's wayward behavior makes the poet dizzy, but he's still scribbling away, nose deep in his papers.

All the while he is keeping watch for a particular young lady. The poet had met her at a dinner party the night before. She is the daughter of a famous painter, and sang so beautifully. Her performance was late in the evening. Johanna is her name. They'd only exchanged a few words, but there was a natural bond between them, the poet felt sure of it. The pale skin, those blue eyes— and she had read his work. *I thanked her, and her cheeks darkened red.*

The poet gets up to look. The brandy plays its part in making his blood rush. As a rule, he does not drink much, but his bedeviled, ever-faithful companion—toothache—has followed in his wake. It's a painful, merciless rendezvous, which is dampened somewhat by the strong drink, but Johanna—so fine, so light—would make it disappear completely!

Now a ripple goes through the crowd. Brandy sloshes over his papers, and the poet must save what can be saved. *Now?* Yes. Now the condemned is coming!

And now they form. Now the words flow:

There's the cart carrying the lad! It takes an eternity to get it up the hill. Gallows Hill may be one of the steepest of the land, but those are strong horses pulling, and a man of obvious experience is at the reins. No, the laborious progress is wholly due to the mass of people vying for a glimpse of the condemned: Niels Nielsen. Fifteen years old. Sentenced for murder and arson. Woe and cursed creaking!

I'm afraid, thinks the poet in that moment the cart passes him.

He has slipped too far behind. He wants to get closer to the scaffold, see what happens within when he sees it. Not *too* close, though. But perhaps Johanna is right up front?

He tries to force his way forward and is immediately swept up by the thrust from behind. He makes a mental note: *My feet have lost contact with the earth, so great is the number. Everything* is shimmering in the sun. There is a slight smell of sulfur in the air, as if the hill led to a smoking volcano, not a scaffold. Beads of sweat are breaking out on my forehead.

He can feel the heat and sweat—his own and that of the masses. People are packed like herrings in a barrel. The nausea rises slowly from his stomach. His arms are wedged to his sides; impossible to write anything down. But he has eyes on stalks, eyes embedded in his head.

You cannot tell from looking at the fifteen-year-old boy that his head will soon be severed from his body. If you didn't know any better, you'd think he was daydreaming. This cannot be said of the rest: The air is nearing boiling point-the masses swelling back and forth!

And yet, some seats are reserved, like at a matinee viewing at the Royal Theatre. Amongst those in the front row are the murdered boy's family. They are treated with a peculiar respect; there's no pushing or shoving in their vicinity. A little circle has formed around them. From here they can look upon and yell at their boy's

murderer; especially mother and sister are
spewing curses at the scaffold. Next to
them the priest is standing in full formal
dress. The mayor is also among those people
who are standing closest to the scaffold,
including a mother and father with their
malformed child. The child seems oblivious
to events. Her head lolls backward onto
the nape of her neck, there are dabs of
spittle around her mouth, but her parents
are determined to let her drink the blood
of the executed boy, in the hope of that
miracle, which will restore the rightful
dignity of their daughter's neck.

I can feel a ripple through my body, thinks the
poet. All the while he sees:

It only seems to agitate the crowd
further that the condemned boy looks like
a lazy apprentice who has sat himself in
the corner to avoid the beady eyes of his
master. Everyone is yelling and spitting on
the lad. A raucous bunch of ruffians have
forced their way to the front row, and
those officers who—up till now—were posted
at the scaffold in all their motionless glory
are suddenly struggling to keep the masses

at bay; their fine uniforms rumpled and clotted with spit in no time.

The boy and the executioner seem to be the only ones taking the proceedings with any measure of dignified calm. The executioner is standing one meter behind the boy, eyes cast down. He is dressed in simple clothing. His hands are hanging down by his sides. Only the scuffle of his feet give him away: *Let's cut to the chase!*

The scaffold is made of a dark, weatherbitten wood—clearly secondhand material—but between the executioner's feet there's a glimpse of an altogether new, pale wood: a newly crafted coffin. To the right of the executioner lies the sack containing the heavy ax. It is an ax that has been passed down for generations; it has done this before. Up close, the boy's face is surprisingly fine, as if he were made of porcelain. As if all the executioner need do is hold him up and drop him—and he'll shatter in a thousand pieces!

A verse occurs to the poet. He mumbles it out loud. To remember it better, taste it:

"A town has many mouths to sate
But only one man in a cape;
Only one ax comes to bear,
One head from its neck to pare."

A fly lands on the poet's nose. Then it's gone.
He thinks: *A messenger of joy—or horror. Of
spring on its way, or the omen of a corpse—which
it will tuck into soon!* As the boy's sentence is
read, the poet thinks of all the horrendous
sicknesses in this world. But when the executioner lifts the ax out of the sack, he is ready.
I'm shaking, the poet thinks. He tunes his body
to the world. *What do you see? What do you
feel? When the executioner braces his legs, raises
his arms; now that he lets the ax fall.*

It is horrible! Quicker than a wink, the executioner severs head and neck. Blood pours out
of the body like a Nordic waterfall! The head,
however, rolls to the far edge of the scaffold, the
staring eyes and yellow tongue are clear to see.
No, the boy was not made of porcelain. And
now there is a patent calm upon the faces of

the sheriff's family. You can see their thoughts rise up to their son with God in heaven, and down to the other in Hell, twisting in flames of eternal, tooth-splintering pain.

Then the poet faints. He falls, and the children scream with laughter. The adults laugh too. The howl of pain shoots up from the base of his spine to the back of his head. He loses his notebook and pen, but finds them again in amongst legs and boots. The crowd gets him back on his feet.

It is not the first time he feels like a foolish fowl. *Thank goodness Johanna didn't see me!* he thinks. *I wouldn't get a moment's sleep if she'd seen me!*

Tomorrow the poet will be on his way. He makes a resolution: *First thing tomorrow morning I'll look her up, that dear girl, and confess my feelings for her. If she feels the same, stay. If not, say adieu—and be away.*

When he sits in a hotel room somewhere in this world, he will write it all down and send it to her.

Will she tremble and cry when she reads his words? Will she long for him when he is thousands of miles away? Or will he be forgotten? Will he be rubbed out from memory? Ah, who knows? To travel is to live!

Now the final words of the letter come to him. The final verse:

> One town's many mouths, a chorus fair,
> Whilst a head that still doth stare
> Rolls to the ground
> Without a sound.

It's not just about that executed boy. She will understand that.

The poet sees it before him, as if he were sitting in the same room. He sees a figure reading a letter in a chair by the window. She looks out the window, hugging his words to her bosom.

The boy has felt, and not felt, the hand that has taken hold of his hair.

"Mississippi."

The boy doesn't know why, but he says it out loud. He tries to count them. He is not good at words, but he keeps trying, till he's as sure, as sure can be: four. There are four *s*'s in that meandering river. But there are also four *i*'s. So there are just as many *i*'s as there are *s*'s; just as many men without heads, he thinks, and dives into the water. That's how it feels when the hand pushes his head down onto the block: like diving headfirst into water.

Now the executioner is swinging his ax, and

the boy is executed on Gallows Hill; the move-
ment is quick and resolute, the head is already
severed from its body, but still it feels like the
age of a mountain; the boy has taken note of
all the people, not that he consciously wished
to block them out—he makes a note of everything and everyone—but he fixes irrationally
long on certain things: A mother, who has dis-
covered a louse in her son's hair, how she rakes
through it, finds the louse, tries to squash it to
death between her fingers; he hears shouting,
many voices yelling, but one voice in particular stands out—it is loud and clear, a young
man calling, "Simon! Simon! Simon!"; he can
smell a particular tobacco that reminds him
of that time when he found a cigarette case on
the road, picked it up, and put it back where
he'd found it—only to turn and see it taken by
another; it ought not be possible, but the boy
is sure he can hear the dog; the hill is black
with people, but again one man stands out—
he twists his upper body, looks down, and lifts
his elbow, and a whine pierces the noise as the

man kicks the dog lying at his feet; the boy realizes that it was right here where he once sat with his father to rest his broken body; finally, he sees a birthmark on the executioner's hand and that the sun is already lower than it stood before. The boy thinks that everything happens so unbelievably slow, yet so unbelievably fast. Also this is something he has felt before:

The river water is surprisingly warm, and he swims easily upstream, with effortless, powerful strokes.

Then there's a thump against the back of his neck as the raft drifts in. He grabs hold of it, crawls up onto it, and lies on his back with his hand under his head; lets himself be led with the stream.

His body dries in no time under the sun. A fly lands on his knee.

The raft drifts gently down the river.

S after S after S.

After the next S,
he catches sight
of the dog on land
three legs and
a wagging tail
he lifts an arm
and waves
with a boy's
hand so slim
and sunburned
into the

next curve
he sees his father
tall and straight
like a soldier
he salutes
before the girl is
on the bank
tousling
her hair
she throws
a flower
red leaves

like a roof
he cannot
grab
hold
of
them
he looks up
she is standing there
and smiling
her hair is
so black
so shiny
that
he still
thinks
there
you
are
before
the
last
swing

Author's Note

On February 22, 1853, fifteen-year-old Niels Nielsen was executed, sentenced to death on charges of arson and murder of the sheriff's little son. It was the last execution in Svendborg, Denmark. Gallows Hill still exists. At the top of the hill there is a bench. From here, you can sit and look down over the town. Just to the right of the hill is a kindergarten, the Parrot, attended by my two sons, Jeppe and Jacob.

atheneum

An imprint of Simon & Schuster Children's Publishing Division • 1230 Avenue of the Americas, New York, New York 10020 • This book is a work of fiction. Any references to historical events, real people, or real places are used fictitiously. Other names, characters, places, and events are products of the author's imagination, and any resemblance to actual events or places or persons, living or dead, is entirely coincidental. • Text copyright © 2010 by Jesper Wung-Sung and Resinante & Co./Host & Son, Copenhagen • Published by agreement with Gyldendal Group Agency • English translation copyright © 2016 by Lindy Falk van Rooyen • Illustrations by Sonia Chaghatzbanian • All rights reserved, including the right of reproduction in whole or in part in any form. • Atheneum logo is a trademark of Simon & Schuster, Inc. • For information about special discounts for bulk purchases, please contact Simon & Schuster Special Sales at 1-866-506-1949 or business@simonandschuster.com. • The Simon & Schuster Speakers Bureau can bring authors to your live event. For more information or to book an event, contact the Simon & Schuster Speakers Bureau at 1-866-248-3049 or visit our website at www.simonspeakers.com. • Also available in an Atheneum hardcover edition • Book design by Sonia Chaghatzbanian and Irene Metaxatos • The text for this book was set in Adobe Jenson Pro. • Manufactured in the United States of America • First Atheneum paperback edition March 2017 • 10 9 8 7 6 5 4 3 2 1 • The Library of Congress has cataloged the hardcover edition as follows: • Names: Wung-Sung, Jesper, 1971– author. | Van Rooyen, Lindy Falk, translator. • Title: The last execution / Jesper Wung-Sung ; translation by Lindy Falk van Rooyen. • Other titles: Sidste henrettelse. English • Description: First edition. | New York : Atheneum Books for Young Readers, [2016] | ?2010 | Originally published in Danish by Host & Son in 2010 under title: Den sidste henrettelse. | Summary: Based on the true story of the last execution in Denmark's history, this novel asks a question that plagues a small Danish town in 1853: does a fifteen-year-old boy deserve to be put to death? • Identifiers: LCCN 2015033461 • ISBN 978-1-4814-2965-8 (hc) • ISBN 978-1-4814-2966-5 (pbk) • ISBN 978-1-4814-2967-2 (eBook) • Subjects: | CYAC: Executions and executioners—Fiction. | Death—Fiction. | Denmark—History—1849–1866—Fiction. • Classification: LCC PZ7.1.W96 Las 2016 | DDC [Fic]—dc23 • LC record available at http://lccn.loc.gov/2015033461